Carley McFarley
AND
Sydney McFinley
(The Mystery of the Vanishing Dogs)

Belinda Ellenberger

outskirts
press

Outskirts Press, Inc.
http://www.outskirtspress.com

ISBN: 978-1-9772-5857-1

Cover Image by Belinda Ellenberger\
Interior Illustrations by Craig Sacra

Outskirts Press and the "OP" logo are trademarks belonging to Outskirts Press, Inc.

PRINTED IN THE UNITED STATES OF AMERICA

CHAPTER 1

Tap, tap, tap. Tap, tap, tap. Sydney ducked back under the covers and pretended that Carley was not tap-tapping on her window.

Sydney slowly peeked one eye out from under the covers and looked at the window; three pairs of eyes stared back at her. As Sydney looked closer, she realized it was her cousin, Carley, with her brindle boxer, Gypsy, and Sydney's yellow Labrador retriever, Jazz.

Slowly, Sydney crawled out of bed and reluctantly opened the window.

She couldn't help but laugh as Carley, Gypsy, and Jazz were all trying to be the first to get through the window.

Sydney took a box of dog treats off the top shelf of her bookcase and gave Gypsy and Jazz each one treat. Then, she motioned for them to go back out the window. Happily, they both obliged.

Once the dogs were safely out the window, Carley turned to Sydney and declared, "I'm here to tell you we have our first real case! Great, huh?"

For the umpteenth time Sydney informed Carley, "I am not going to be a private investigator."

Carley and Sydney are cousins, best friends, and neighbors. During the construction of their new homes, Sydney and Carley both had birthdays. Sydney reached her teen years; she turned a whopping thirteen years old. Carley made twelve.

When Carley was born, her grandmother started calling her Carley McFarley, and the name stuck. Carley started calling Sydney Sydney McFinley, and again, the name stuck. They are now known as Carley McFarley and Sydney McFinley by practically everyone.

Until recently, their homes were near a swamp. The swamp was full of alligators, snakes, opossums, raccoons, and all sorts of weird critters. Carley and Sydney discovered the secrets of the glowing lights in the swamp and were forced to move.

Now, they live in a large subdivision. All the homes in the subdivision are on three-acre lots. Sydney's grandparents' home is the tenth house on the right. Sydney's parents' home is next, and the twelfth house is Carley's parents. Part of Carley's parents' property goes around the circle.

Carley keeps insisting that when she and Sydney grow up, they are going to be private investigators.

She even has the name of their company picked out: McFarley's Private Investigation Firm. Sydney keeps insisting that Carley's dream is not happening.

"You'll change your mind when you hear Laura's story. We have to help her. She came all this way," stated Carley.

"I don't know what you are even talking about, Carley. Who's Laura and where is she? You said she came all this way," said Sydney.

Carley widened her eyes, and guiltily whispered, "She's outside the window."

"Outside the window? Are you crazy? Why do you have a girl outside my window?"

Sydney stuck her head out the window and saw a petite little girl standing close by the side of the house. Tears were streaming down her cheeks as she looked at Sydney. The girl had dark skin and large dark brown eyes. Her black hair looked like, at one time, it had been pulled neatly on top of her head and secured with a ponytail holder. Now, the ponytail holder was gone and her hair was sticking up in all directions. She was wearing torn, dirty pajamas and mud-caked tennis shoes with no socks.

Sydney asked the little girl, "What are you doing here?"

The little girl was now sobbing as she answered, "I'm Laura."

"So," said Sydney, "I still don't know why you are here."

"Quit being mean to her," demanded Carley.

Still looking at Laura, Sydney insisted, "I'm not being mean. I just want to know why she's here."

Sydney turned angrily to Carley. "You wake me up at six o'clock on a Saturday morning when I could be sleeping late. There's a girl outside my window, and I don't know why."

Sydney put her hands on her hips and demanded, "Okay, Carley. What's going on?"

Carley lightly bumped Sydney from the window and turned to Laura. "It's okay, Laura. You can come in now. I'll help you; just give me your hands."

With trembling lips and tears still running down her cheeks, Laura said, "No. She don't like me. She won't help."

Carley turned and glared at Sydney with her mean eyes. Sydney folded her arms in front of her and just stood there.

"I promise, Laura, she'll help when she hears your story. She loves animals more than anybody; she's just cranky in the morning. Come on, give me your hands and I'll help you in."

Laura, still crying, held her hands out to Carley, and Carley helped her into Sydney's bedroom.

Sydney looked at the dirt on Laura and on her muddy shoes. She thought about how much trouble she was going to be in if her mom saw all the mud on the floor, not to mention the windowsill.

"Before we do anything," said Sydney, "we have to get you cleaned up. First, take off the shoes and throw them out the window. Carley, bring her to the bathroom and wipe her face and hands. I know I have some clothes that might fit her that I out-grew. Mom hasn't cleaned out my closet in ages."

Carley took off Laura's shoes and threw them out the window. Then, she led Laura to the bathroom and had her wash her hands and face. Sydney brought the clothes for Laura to wear: a pink T-shirt, a pair of blue jeans, and a brand-new pair of socks.

Once Laura had the clothes, Sydney said, "We'll leave you in here so you can change. When you are finished, come back to my bedroom."

Once Carley and Sydney got back into Sydney's bedroom, Sydney made a slicing motion to her throat and gave Carley the "You are in so much trouble" look. Carley pretended not to notice. Within a few minutes, Laura came back to the bedroom with her dirty and tattered clothes draped on her arm. Her hair was sticking up in all directions, but she still looked cute.

Sydney asked Laura, "Do you want me to braid your hair? I know how."

Laura sadly said, "No. I want you to find Jolie." She reached into the pocket of her dirty pants and dug out a crumpled $10 bill. "I have money," she whispered. "I can pay."

"Who's Jolie?" asked Sydney.

Carley explained, "Jolie is Laura's dog and she wants us to find her."

"Do you know what happened to her?" Sydney asked.

"A boy stole her," cried Laura. "Grandma said I left the gate open and she ran away. No she didn't. I saw her. A white boy in an old truck stole her."

"Did you see anything else?" asked Sydney.

"She's visiting her grandma," explained Carley. "She brought her dog with her. She let her out to do her business and when she went to let her back in, she saw a boy put the dog in his truck. This was yesterday evening."

Sydney glanced sideways at Carley. "Really? I thought Laura was going to tell me the story."

"Well, I figured I'd tell you since she gets so upset," said Carley.

Sydney opened up her desk drawer and withdrew two ink pens and two note pads. She gave a pen and note pad to Carley.

"I'm going to ask you some questions," Sydney said to Laura. "I want you to answer, not Carley."

"Okay," sniffed Laura.

"What time was it when you let out Jolie?"

"Yesterday. Just before supper. Grandma told me to let her out to use the bathroom and I did."

"Did you put her on a chain?" asked Sydney.

"No," said Carley. "Her grandma has a fenced in backyard."

Sydney glared at Carley, "Carrrrrrley!"

"Sorry," she said.

Sydney turned her attention back to Laura. "Was the gate latched?"

"Yes," said Laura. "I always make sure the gate is latched. I don't want her to get out; she's my best friend."

"You saw the boy take Jolie out of your yard?" asked Sydney.

"No. I saw him put her in a cage in the back of his truck," answered Laura.

As Sydney was gathering her clothes for the day she said, "We'll take you back to your grandma and try to find out what's going on."

Sydney brought her clothes into the bathroom. After washing her face, brushing her teeth and her hair, she felt human again.

When she walked back into her bedroom Carley and Laura was sitting on the edge of her bed. Neither one was speaking. Laura's head kept bobbing up and down. Her eyes were closed.

Sydney asked, "Carley, do you know where she lives?"

"No," answered Carley.

"You can't let her fall asleep. We don't know where to take her."

Carley shook Laura and asked, "Where do you live, Laura?"

"Baton Rouge," Laura groggily answered.

"I mean your grandma. Where does your grandma live?" asked Sydney.

With a wide yawn, Laura said, "Maple Street."

"I know where that is," stated Carley. "You just go down Adams Road and you take a right on Maple Street."

"You can't get there unless you cross the main highway. She can't do that; it's too dangerous. She could get run over. How did she get to your house?"

Carley answered, "She said she walked."

"That's too far for her to walk."

"Well, duh. I know it. But she did it anyway. That's why she's so tired."

They looked toward Laura. She was curled into a little ball, soundly sleeping.

"Do you know how many houses are on Maple Street?" asked Sydney.

"Lots," stated Carley. "Let's text Cole and see if he can drive us. You can buy him breakfast."

They looked toward Laura. She was curled into a little ball soundly sleeping

CHAPTER 2

"Me, buy him breakfast? How about you buying him breakfast."

Carley insisted, "I don't have money. Laura just gave you $10. You work and have money."

"I don't work that much. Aunt Crystal only works me every now and then. She said she'll work me more hours during the summer."

"Well, it's summer now," declared Carley.

"Give me a break, Carley. School just ended yesterday. I don't get my hours until Monday."

While they were bickering, Carley was texting Cole. Normally they would have called their cousin, Paul, but Paul had been busy with his lawn service business. Cole agreed to meet them in front of Sydney's house. Cole informed Carley that she had to buy him breakfast. Carley texted back, agreeing.

Within a few minutes, Cole pulled up in front of Sydney's house in his old beat-up white Ford Explorer. His dad gave it to him when he bought himself a new Dodge Charger right after Cole's sister, Melissa, started college.

Cole was fifteen, tall for his age with red hair and green eyes, and slightly overweight. He was excited when his dad gave him the family's old Ford Explorer. It came with a promise that when Cole started college he would get a new car like he gave Melissa when she started college.

Sydney picked up Laura and thought, *She's as light as a feather.*

As Sydney was heading out the front door with Laura, Carley headed to the kitchen. Cole watched as Sydney sat Laura into the seat behind the passenger seat and fastened the seat belt. She reclined the seat slightly to make Laura more comfortable. Sydney got into the seat next to Laura.

Carley opened the passenger's door. As she was fastening her seat belt, she gave Cole a pack of Pop-Tarts.

Cole made a face and asked, "What's this?"

"It's your breakfast," replied Carley.

Cole said, "I don't want this. I want a real breakfast."

"We don't have time for a real breakfast. We have to get to Maple Street. You do know where Maple Street is, right?"

Cole gave her in indignant look as he said, "Of course. Even if I didn't, my phone does have GPS. You do know that, right? By the way, you owe me a McDonald's big breakfast."

Maple Street was four miles from their subdivision. Sydney was amazed that Laura had walked to Carley's house. Sydney asked Carley, "How did she even know where you lived?"

Carley answered, "I asked her that when I answered the door. She said her grandma drove through our subdivision yesterday and told her that a real smart girl lives in that house. That's why she came to my house. Because I'm smart."

Sydney rolled her eyes.

Cole stated, "Her grandma must be mentally challenged."

Carley opened her mouth to say something, but Cole pulled onto Maple Street. He stopped on the side of the street and asked, "Which house?"

Sydney and Carley stared at the abundance of homes lining both sides of the street. Carley turned sideways in her seat, looked at Sydney, and Sydney shrugged her shoulders.

Cole asked, "You do know where she lives, right?"

Carley answered, "I just know that her grandma lives on Maple Street. Laura's visiting her grandma for a week. I didn't know it had these many houses," explained Carley.

Cole explained, "The man that built these houses named the streets after trees. He built a bunch of streets. Maple Street is the first street he built. After he builds a house, he plants a tree in the backyard by the property line. If you live on Maple Street you get a maple tree. If you live on Cedar Wood Street you get…"

"All right, all right," said Sydney. "That's real interesting, but it doesn't help us in finding Laura's grandma."

"How do you know all this?" asked Carley.

"Paul told me. I help him sometimes. He's getting a lot of work. Sometimes he asks me to help him when he's real busy. He's hoping to get a lot of business in this area."

Sydney said, "That's great, Cole. Carley, did she say anything about her grandma's house?"

Carley stated, "She was only talking about her dog. We have to find her dog. She's really upset. We know her grandma has a fenced-in backyard."

"Look, Carley! Almost every house on the street has a fenced in backyard. How are we going to find her dog when we can't even find the house?"

Carley looked at Sydney and flatly stated, "Ah, jeez. You are so negative today."

"Wake her up," said Cole.

Carley said, "But she's sleeping so peacefully. I hate to disturb her."

While Carley was speaking, Sydney had unlatched Laura's seatbelt and whispered in Laura's ear, "Wake up. You have to tell us where your grandma lives."

Laura opened her eyes, looked at Sydney, and fell back to sleep.

"She won't wake up," said Sydney. "She is really out of it."

Cole opened the windows and turned off the motor.

"What are you doing?" Sydney asked.

"I'm going to sit here and eat my Pop- Tarts." He tore open the pop tart package, took out one Pop-Tart, and started eating.

"It's too hot," complained Carley. "You can at least leave the air conditioner on."

Cole replied, "Excuse me. You are crazy if you think I'm going to leave the air on for two Pop-Tarts. Besides, this is an old vehicle that has to last me a long time."

In response, Carley stuck her tongue out at him. She turned to Sydney and said, "I guess we can go to the houses and ask if Laura's grandma lives there. We know her name is Ann, and she lives on Maple Street. The houses are real close together. It looks like the street is only about a half mile long."

CHAPTER 3

Sydney assigned herself the houses on the left and Carley took the houses on the right. Sydney walked onto the porch of a small brick house. The porch extended from one corner of the house to the next. The porch was decorated with a small black wrought-iron glider and two white chairs. Several flower pots with marigolds and multicolored petunias took up a large portion of the porch. The area was so peaceful that Sydney resisted the urge to sit down and watch Carley across the street. Sydney thought, *Real nice people must live here.* Reluctantly, she raised her hand to knock on the door. Suddenly, the door opened and she almost hit a lady in the face.

The lady had her light-brown hair pulled up in a bun. She wore a light-brown business suit and had keys in one hand and a light-brown purse in the other hand. Her high-heeled shoes matched her purse. She looked at Sydney as though she was an irritating gnat.

"What do you want? I don't have time for nonsense. I have to get to work. And I don't want any cookies."

For a moment Sydney couldn't utter a word. She stood there with her mouth opened. She couldn't remember what she had to ask. The lady looked at her for a split second then started down the steps toward the one car carport.

Sydney regained her thought process and scurried down the steps after the lady. In doing so, she missed the bottom step and landed on her knees.

The lady turned around and demanded, "Why are you still here? You need to leave."

"I just have one question, ma'am."

"One question and make it snappy. I told you, I'm on my way to work."

Sydney spoke so quickly her words ran together. "Do you know a woman by the name of Ann who lives down this street? It's really important. It's about her granddaughter, Laura."

"Never heard of her. Now leave!"

The lady reached her car, unlocked the door, sat behind the wheel, and drove away without another glance at Sydney.

Sydney thought, *Yeah, some really nice people must live here.*

Sydney took her notebook and wrote: First house on the left, nothing. Did not know Ann.

Sydney proceeded to the next house. Before knocking, she glanced over her shoulder to see Carley. Carley was speaking to a man at the first house she went to.

I hope she has better luck than me, thought Sydney.

Sydney went up the steps to the second house. No one answered the door. Sydney wrote in her notebook: Second house, no one answered.

Then she went to the third house and knocked on that door. An elderly man with grey hair and wearing only a Speedo opened the door. He gave Sydney a huge smile as he said, "May I help you, little lady?"

Again Sydney was rendered speechless. She forgot what she had to ask him. "Um, umm."

"Yes, what is it?" he asked.

She remembered what she had to ask. "Do you know a lady down this street by the name of Ann?"

The man put his right index finger to his mouth. His eyes were looking upward as he was thinking.

Finally, he said, "No. Sorry, can't help you. Don't know Ann."

Sydney thanked him and hurriedly left the house. She pulled out her notebook and wrote: "Third house, man answered door; doesn't know Ann."

By the time she reached the fourth house she was getting tired, hungry, and thirsty. She wrote in her notebook: "Fourth house, man slammed door in my face."

She still had no luck at all by the time she reached the eighth house. She glanced across the street to see how Carley was doing. Carley was missing. *Where's Carley*? Thought Sydney. She started getting worried, and thinking some nut took Carley. Sydney raced across the street and began searching the front yards of the houses.

When Sydney reached the third house on the right, she saw Carley on the porch of the second house drinking iced tea, eating cookies and socializing with an elderly woman. *I'm working and Carley is being entertained.*

She angrily went to the front of the house, put on her smiley face and sarcastically said, "Hi, Carley. How are you doing?"

"Hi," said Carley. This is Ms. Sanders."

Carley turned to Ms. Sanders and said, "This is my cousin, Sydney. She's the one I was telling you about. She's helping me find Ms. Ann."

Then Carley turned to Sydney, "Ms. Sanders knows about another missing dog. She said a friend of hers on Redwood Street lost her white and tan pit bull."

"That's right," stated Ms. Sanders. "My friend, Joyce, had her pit bull in her yard. When she came out to get Brutus, he was gone. The gate was opened. She was positive it was closed when she let Brutus out in the yard. But she couldn't swear to it. She was letting him in and out all day. When she let him out that evening he wasn't in the yard, and the gate was open. Joyce is very upset. She felt protected with him in the house."

"When was that?" asked Sydney.

"About two evenings ago," said Ms. Sanders. "Oh, Sydney, please forgive my bad manners; would you like some tea and cookies?"

Sydney said, "Yes, thank ..."

Carley interrupted, "No, thank you. She doesn't have time. We have to be on our way. Thank you, though. And thank you for my tea and cookies."

Carley turned to go and said, "Come on, Sydney. We have work to do."

Sydney followed her to the street. "Well, thanks, Carley. I was thirsty, you know. You only made it to the second house. I've already been to seven."

"Cool," said Carley. "What did you find out? Do you know where Laura's grandma lives?"

"No," stated Sydney. "Either no one was home, or they didn't know Ann. Except for the fourth house." She looked at her notes. "The man slammed the door in my face. The lady in house number five told me she didn't want anything and shut the door. So, I've been having a real nice day."

Carley looked at her notes. "Well, the man in the first house I went to said a friend of his across town was missing a terrier. He said the man was really mad. He thinks a coyote jumped over the fence and got his dog. The dog was there one minute and the next it vanished. That's why he thinks it's a coyote. He said coyotes are fast like that."

"Ewww, how horrible," stated Sydney.

"That's what I say. We still have to find Ms. Ann. Maybe Laura woke up. Let's go check."

As they were walking to the Ford Explorer, three police cars passed them.

"Wow! Where do you think they are going?" Carley asked.

The police cars stopped in front of a house many houses down. Sydney looked at Carley and said, "I bet that's Ms. Ann's house. She probably discovered Laura's missing."

"Oh, no. We're going to be arrested," said Carley.

"No, we are not," assured Sydney. Let's go see. If that isn't Ms. Ann's house, we have to tell the police about Laura. They'll help us find her grandma."

They walked while they spoke. When they reached the house, they saw a distraught and crying lady. She had brown skin and black and silver hair. A red robe was covering her pajamas. She was talking to two police officers. One police officer was an av- erage- height woman. She wore black-rimmed glasses and had short black hair. She had a clipboard in her hand taking notes. The other police officer was a tall, skinny woman with brown hair pulled into a small ponytail. Carley and Sydney walked past two police officers searching the yard.

When they got to the lady, Carley said, "Excuse me, ma'am."

The lady wiped tears off her cheeks, stared at Carley, then looked at Sydney. Carley continued speaking, "Are you Ms. Ann, Laura's grandma?"

They lady's eyes widened. "Yes, I am. Do you know any- thing about my granddaughter? Do you know where she is?"

"Yes, ma'am. She came to my house early this morning. She fell asleep before she could tell us where you live. She just said Maple Street."

While Carley was speaking with Ms. Ann, Sydney called Cole and told him to bring his Explorer by the police cars and bring Laura.

"Where is she now?" Ann wailed.

Sydney looked toward the street and said, "Here she is. We had Cole drive us ..."Ann didn't wait for Sydney to finish. She ran to the Explorer and grabbed Laura out of Cole's hands.

The tall police officer looked aggravated when she demanded, "Explain what's going on here."

Carley explained, "She showed up at my house early this morning and I went to Sydney's house."

"Yes," said Sydney. "At six o'clock to be exact. And this was the morning I could sleep late."

Carley gave Sydney her mean look, rolled her eyes, and said, "Oh, pleeeese. Laura asked us to find her dog, Jolie."

The tall police officer said, "Why did she go to your house, and where do you live?"

One of the police officers (an average- height male with a dark-brown crew cut) searching the yard came over and said, "I know them. Those are the two girls that caused the government to close that road to the swamp. Remember me telling you about them, Barbara?" Barbara was the short female police officer.

"Oh, yes," she said. "They were the talk of the town for a while."

After Carley finished telling them about Laura's early-morning visit and them being determined to help Laura find her dog, the officers wished them the best, and left.

On the way to the car, the male officer said to Barbara, "I bet you $50 they are going to find the kid's dog."

Barbara said, "No way. Not taking you up on that one."

Ann ushered Cole, Sydney, and Carley into her living room. The living room looked cozy. An almond-colored plush sofa set was centered against a wall, facing a wall with a flat-screen television set. End tables were on each side of the sofa. One end table had a laptop computer, and the other end table had an adult coloring book with colored pencils. After putting Laura into bed, Ms. Ann came into the living room and thanked them for returning Laura.

Carley asked, "Do you know of anyone else missing a dog?"

Ms. Ann informed them that she did not.

Before leaving, Sydney said, "Please tell Laura that we will do everything we can to find Jolie. When we find her, we will call you."

Ms. Ann handed a $20 bill to Carley and thanked them again.

Walking to the Ford Explorer, Cole snatched the $20 bill from Carley and said, "Gas and food."

Carley and Sydney both made a face at Cole. Sydney said, "I know you keep water in here, Cole. Give me a bottle, then you can leave. We'll call you when we're finished talking with the neighbors."

Cole opened the back of the Explorer and gave each girl a bottle of water. "I'm going to get a big breakfast and go home. Call me when you are ready for me to pick you up."

After he left, Sydney pulled out her notebook and discussed the next step. They continued interviewing as many people as possible; it was way past lunchtime by the time they were finished. They were both tired and hungry. Carley called Cole. He picked them up and drove them back to Sydney's house.

She saw Carley on the porch of the second house drinking iced tea, eating cookies and socializing with an elderly woman.

CHAPTER 4

After hurriedly eating a ham and cheese sandwich, the girls went into the craft room to compare notes. Sydney's mom, Stacy, had a large 4'X6' dry-erase board attached to the wall. That's where Stacy wrote her to-do lists. That's also where she wrote Sydney's list of chores.

"Let's go through our notebooks and I'll write down anything the people said that might help."

"Let's take one street at a time," said Carley.

Sydney wrote the names of all the streets they had been to that day. When they completed listing the information they gathered this is what they had:

Maple Street on Right:
1. 1st house—man across town missing a dog
2. 9th house – Ms. Ann, Laura's dog disappeared Friday evening – black labradoodle, Jolie – white boy in old white truck
3. 12th house – Ms. Martin, missing a brown Chihuahua, Buddy, disappeared early Thursday morning
4. 14th house – no dog missing, Mr. Graham saw old white Ford pick-up truck almost every morning between five-thirty to six o'clock; did not have good view of driver

Maple Street on Left:
1. 10th house – Ms. Lewis, missing black and tan 20-pound mutt, named Jack – disappeared Tuesday

Cedar Wood Street on Right:
1. 5th house – Ms. Hayes, her friend, Jane Pines, across town on Hoover Rd had two hunting dogs vanish overnight. Husband told wife he saw a bright light in the back yard. The dogs vanished. Believes aliens took his dogs for experiments.
2. 6th house – Will Boyd, seeing brown car driving up and down the street for days – weird
3. 10th house – Ms. Ball, her friend, Janet, lives one mile down Adams Road, missing a white pit bull, Dolly
4. 14th house – Mr. Nolan, black and white Austrian Shepherd mixed, missing since early morning Monday
5. 7th house – Mr. Steward, missing a terrier mix, since Monday morning

Cedar Wood Street on Left:
1. No one answered the doors for Sydney

Cypress Street Right:
1. 5th house – Mr. Ralph, saw boy driving real slow in old white Ford pick-up truck – white boy with dirty, greasy, shoulder length hair – thought he was looking for work
2. 10th house – Ms. Nancy, missing her German shepherd puppy. Puppy is four months old, missing since this Saturday morning (today) could not find her puppy. Let puppy out, went to get coffee, just vanished—no trace
3. 11th house – Ms. Neal, friend of Ms. Nancy, heard a noise, looked out her window, and saw a young man get into an old white truck and drive off – did not know Ms. Nancy's puppy was missing until Nancy came to her house crying
4. 14th house – Ms. Fletcher, sits on porch and crochets all the

time – been noticing a nice brown Nissan Maxima driving up and down the streets going real slow – been seeing it often

Cypress Street Left
1. 7th house – Ms. Jackson, saw old white truck with a pit bull in back in a kennel, can't remember when she saw it

Redwood Street Right
1. 1. 4th house – Ms. Joyce, tan and white pit bull, Brutus, disappeared out her yard Wednesday evening
2. 10th house – Ms. Susan, has been noticing a brown Nissan Maxima going slow in front of her house – she owns a boxer, named Judd
3. 13th house – Ms. Beverly, boxer Tank, went missing Tuesday night around eight o'clock, went to bring him in and he just vanished – gates were still shut
4. 14th house – Mr. Ned, does not have a dog, but has been seeing an old white pick-up truck being driven up and down the street

Redwood Street Left
1. 3rd house – Ms. Campbell's Rottweiler, named Scout, went missing Thursday night; Scout is 6 months old

Oakwood Street Right
1. 1st house – Ms. Dorothy-- her friend-- Marianne, across town, is missing a white and tan shih tzu mix, named George, lives on Hoover Road. Marianne thinks aliens came down and took her dog
2. 6th house – Ms. Donna, her friend Mattie lives across town, missing a boxer, Buttercup, been missing almost two weeks – lives on Hoover Road – Reward

3. 11th house – Ms. Gayle, her dog, Puff, missing since Tuesday, a fluffy white Pomeranian – reward $500 – put in paper
4. 12th house – Mr. Blackwell and his wife, does not have dogs – noticing an old white Ford pick-up truck with a young man driving – took down license plate number

Oak Street Left
1. No one on left side gave Sydney any information

"Okay, now let's make a plan with what we have," said Sydney. "What do you think about the people thinking aliens from outer space took their dogs?"

Carley stated, "I think they must be related to my Maw Maw. I called Maw Maw last night and told her about our case. She said it is probably aliens taking the dogs. Is that all you were able to get, Sydney?"

"That's all," said Sydney. "The people either weren't home or they slammed the door in my face."

"Why would they do that? You have such a sunny personality," Carley said sarcastically.

"I know. Right? I don't know why people are so mean to me."

Carley shook her head and rolled her eyes.

Sydney gave an eye roll to Carley and said, "Well, nobody can be as peeerrrfect as Ms. Car ..."

"Sydney, come and eat. Supper is ready," Stacy said, as she stepped into the craft room.

"Carley, are you eating here or going home?" Stacy asked.

"I have to go home. I have to eat and take a bath bomb bath. It's been a long day. I'll come back later."

Carley left, and Sydney went into the kitchen to eat supper.

CHAPTER 5

Sydney was sitting at the craft table writing notes when she heard a tap, tap tapping on the window. Without opening up the blinds she asked, "Who's there?"

"It's me, Carley. Let me in."

Carley's eyes opened wide when suddenly the blinds were pulled up, and she stared into Aunt Stacy's eyes.

"Carley, how many times do I have to tell you to stop coming in through the windows. There are doors you can come through," Stacy fussed.

"Well, I didn't want to bother ..."

Her words were lost when they heard a loud yowl from Gypsy. Jazz was viciously barking.

Stacy and Sydney were knocking each other over trying to get out of the window first. Carley ran to Gypsy just as Gypsy hit the ground. Jazz barked at the gate.

Carley started to yell, scream and cry, "Get up Gypsy. Get up! Help, Aunt Stacy! Somebody shot Gypsy! Gypsy, Gypsy!"

Carley sat on the ground and held Gypsy's head in her hand. Stacy ran to Gypsy and knelt beside her. "Give me your flashlight, Carley," demanded Stacy.

Carley gave Stacy her flashlight. As Stacy was checking Gypsy, she found a dart protruding out of Gypsy's side. She removed the dart and said, "Somebody shot Gypsy with a dart ..."

She stopped speaking when Carley let out a horrific scream and started running. Sydney jumped up and ran after Carley. Carley ran through the gate that separated their yards. She ran through the gate that led to her front yard; and she ran through her front yard to the road. She was running after an old white pick-up truck.

The truck speeded off onto the highway. Carley was forced to stop.

By the time Stacy and Sydney reached Carley, they were all out of breath.

Gasping, Carley said, "Did you see him, Sydney? You saw him, huh, Aunt Stacy? It's the same truck everyone's keeps seeing. He killed Gypsy." Carley started to cry again.

Stacy said, "No, Carley. He knocked her out with a dart. Let's call Aunt Crystal. She'll tell us if we have to bring her to the emergency vet clinic."

Stacy walked back to her house to get her phone. While she was telling her Aunt Crystal about the dart in Gypsy's side Carley and Sydney were petting Gypsy. They were talking to her quietly. Jazz was standing over Gypsy whining.

Within a few minutes, Crystal was there. Using her flashlight she kept in her purse, Crystal examined Gypsy's eyes. Then, she examined her gums and her breathing.

Carley and Sydney told her everything that happened during the day and about the guy in the beat-up old white truck.

While they were telling the story, Tracey and Cliff (Carley's mom and dad) noticed a light in the yard and went outside to see what was happening. Carley and Sydney had to repeat the story to them.

Before Crystal left, she said, "I'm going to go on Neighborhood Watch and alert everyone. I'll tell them to watch their dogs. I didn't realize they had dogs missing." She told the girls to bring the dogs inside and for them not to let the dogs outside unattended.

"You better not go outside alone either. If they can steal dogs, they can steal you. Oh, and don't forget. Sydney, you are on the schedule for seven o'clock tomorrow morning. Stacy, make sure she gets up. No excuse for being late."

"I'll be there, Aunt Crystal. I promise," assured Sydney.

Their Aunt Crystal, Stacy's mom's little sister, was a vet tech for nineteen years before she opened her own Pet Sitting Service. It was called Pet Pal Pet Sitting Service. She boarded all sorts of animals including birds, cats, dogs, and guinea pigs. One time she even boarded a couple of goats. She won't board spiders. She hates spiders. Sydney works for her sometimes when needed. Christine, Crystal's daughter, works for her; she also had two other workers.

Cliff picked up Gypsy to bring her inside their home. Carley asked her mom, "Can I go to Sydney's for a little while longer? We have to figure out what we are going to do tomorrow. I think we'll make flyers."

Tracey said, "Just make sure you call me before you come back home so I can watch for you."

Carley promised she would.

During all the running, Carley somehow lost her slippers. She had already taken her bath. She went to Sydney's wearing her pajamas and slippers.

Stacy held the flashlight while they searched for Carley's slippers. All three laughed when they saw Jazz carrying one of the slippers and dropping it in front of Carley.

After finding the other slipper, Stacy said, "Now, let's go inside. I'm tired. I have to take a shower and go to bed."

As they reached the door, Stacy said, "Oh, no. The doors are locked, and I don't have my key. Which one of you is going to go through the window and open the front door?"

"I can't," whined Carley. My foot hurts. I think I stepped on a rock. You go, Sydney."

"Oh, jeez, Carley. When does anything stop you from climbing in my window?"

Carley looked like she was going to start crying again, so, Sydney hurried up and said, "Okay, I'll climb in the window."

Once Sydney had the door opened, Stacy went to her bathroom for a long shower, and then to bed.

Sydney and Carley went into the craft room. They sat at the table, looked over all the material they had accumulated, and made a plan.

Carley sat on the ground and held Gypsy's head in her hand.

CHAPTER 6

Sydney called Paul and whispered, "Paul. I need you to come over now. It's urgent. You're not busy, are you?"

Paul said, "No. I'm just watching television. I had a hard work day today and I'm resting. What's wrong?"

"What makes you think something is wrong?"

Paul replied, "Something is always wrong with you and Carley. You're always needing something."

Sydney went for the compliment tactic. "That's because, other than your dad, you are the smartest person I know. You know how to search things on the computer. You have programs for everything. We don't. We need you to track down the owner of a white Ford pick-up truck. We have the license plate number. You can do that, right?"

"Maybe," he said. "But I'd rather look it up here. Just give me the number."

Sydney gave Paul the license plate number. Paul said, "I'll call you tomorrow morning with the information, if I can get it."

Sydney didn't argue. She knew Paul would come through. He always did.

Carley and Sydney agreed that they couldn't do anything else at this time. They were both tired. Sydney had to get up early to work at Aunt Crystal's. It was time for Carley to go home.

Carley called her mom, then went home to take a shower and get into bed.

Sydney took a shower, set her alarm for six-thirty, and climbed into bed. She fell asleep even before her head hit the pillow.

CHAPTER 7

At exactly six-thirty, Sydney's phone alarm buzzed. Reluctantly, she turned it off and got out of bed. Hurriedly, she dressed. Her mom drove her to Aunt Crystal's to do her work. Sydney let the dogs out, cleaned their kennels while they played, and put fresh food and water (of course with ice) in their bowls. When they were finished playing and ready to eat, she brought them back inside.

She went inside to tell Aunt Crystal she was finished. Aunt Crystal looked extremely tired. Sydney asked, "What's wrong, Aunt Crystal?"

"Nothing, Sydney. I just need a break! I'm thinking about taking a few days off and letting Christine handle it for a while."

"Okay," replied Sydney.

Crystal asked, "By the way, how is Gypsy this morning?"

Sydney answered, "I don't know. I haven't heard from Carley yet."

Paul pulled up just before Sydney walked out of the front door. Crystal yelled, "Don't forget, Sydney. You have to be at work Tuesday morning."

"I know," replied Sydney. "I'll be here."

During the ride home, Paul handed Sydney a slip of paper with the name and address of the owner of the Ford pick-up truck. "His name is Ted Brandson of Loranger," stated Paul.

"Are you ready for a road trip?" Sydney asked.

"Not today," said Paul. "I have two big yards to cut today."

Sydney said, "Well, maybe Cole will take us."

"No, he won't," said Paul. "He's helping me with the yards."

"That's just great!" Sydney said, as Paul pulled up to her house.

Once inside, Sydney took a quick shower, and hurriedly washed her hair. She was ready to go with her parents to the eleven o'clock church service.

After the service, and while her mom and dad were talking with other churchgoers, Sydney spoke with a few herself. She discovered that two other dogs were missing. They both were missing from Easterbrook Road. One dog was a beagle, and the other one was a black terrier.

Back at Sydney's home, Sydney and Carley sat at the craft table and developed a plan. Carley called Cole and convinced him to be their driver for Monday. They were going to spy on Ted Brandson.

CHAPTER 8

Early Monday morning, Sydney jumped out of bed, got dressed, and sat down for breakfast.

Her mom informed her that Briggs was coming over to visit. "Heather has a gift certificate for an all-day spa. She wants to use it before it expires. Briggs wanted to come spend the day with you, and I said, sure."

"Okay," said Sydney. She didn't tell her mom that they were planning to spy on Ted Brandson.

Briggs showed up just as Sydney was finishing her scrambled eggs and toast. Briggs raced into the house and gave Stacy, and then Sydney, a hug.

Briggs excitedly said, "It's been so long since I've seen you, Sydney. What are we going to do? Can Landon come over?"

Laughing, Sydney said, "Sure. I'll call and check. We have to wait on Carley. She's coming over. We have to do some work."

Briggs smile turned into a frown. "Work. I thought we would do something fun."

"We are," said Sydney. "Don't we always have fun?"

Briggs grinned, "Yeah!"

Briggs is the son of Heather and Kyle. He has blond hair just like his mom's. He is six years old. He has one little brother and two little sisters. Kyle is Stacy's cousin, and the son of Darlene, Stacy's dad's sister. Stacy's dad has a big family. Cousins, aunts, and uncles are everywhere.

Stacy left to go to work. "I should be back around four o'clock. If you need anything, just call. Don't open the crock pot. I have a roast in it, and I want it cooked when I get back. Understood?"

Sydney said, "Understood, Mom, bye."

"Can I turn on the TV?" Briggs asked.

"Sure, but we should be leaving soon," answered Sydney.

She thought, *Carley should be here any minute.*

At ten o'clock, Sydney was getting worried. *Carley should have been here by now*, she thought.

Sydney turned to Briggs and said, "Let's walk to Carley's. She should have been here by now. We'll see what's keeping her."

"Sure," said Briggs.

He wasn't watching television anyway. He was playing fetch with Jazz. Jazz and Briggs were both happy to take the game outdoors.

When Sydney reached Carley's house, she noticed her Aunt Tracey's car was still there. *Something is wrong*, she thought. She held her hand up to knock, but hesitated. Sydney was afraid. She looked at Briggs and Jazz. They were still playing fetch. She called them over to stand by her. Sydney again put her hand up to knock. Briggs and Jazz glanced up at her.

What's wrong?" Briggs asked.

"Nothing," she answered.

Sydney held her breath and softly knocked twice. No answer. She knocked twice again.

Carley opened the door halfway and put her index finger to her mouth to motion for them to be quiet.

Jazz didn't know how to be quiet. She barreled past Carley and looked for Gypsy. Gypsy came running, and squeaking her squeak toy. The squeaking stuffed chicken looked like it definitely had seen better days. Jazz and Gypsy started playing tug of war with the stuffed chicken. Briggs joined in the game.

Sydney whispered to Carley, "What's wrong?"

"I don't know," whispered Carley. "Mom's on the phone

with Aunt Crystal. Aunt Crystal is upset about something. We have to wait until Mom gets off the phone."

A few minutes later Tracey came into the living room.

"Do you know what crazy Aunt Crystal did?"

Carley and Sydney looked at each other. They shook their heads and shrugged their shoulders.

Sydney said, "She's always doing something. What did she do now?"

"Well," Tracey said. "This morning she admitted herself to Harmony Acres."

"That sounds nice," said Carley.

"Yeah," agreed Sydney. "She needed a vacation. She said she was going to take a break. What's wrong with that? Poor Aunt Crystal, can't even go on a little vacation."

Tracey yelled, "It isn't a vacation home. It's an insane asylum."

Sydney and Carley started laughing. Their hands went to their mouths to try to hold back the laughter. They laughed so hard their stomachs ached.

"It isn't funny," said Tracey. "Now, she expects somebody to get her out of there. She thought Harmony Acres was a peaceful resort with massages, spas, and saunas. She wanted the full treatment. She got it alright. Once she found out what she got herself into she wanted out. They won't let her out. She just used her one phone call for the day. I'm calling Granny Nanny to see about hiring an attorney. How does your Aunt Crystal get herself into these situations? I'll tell you how. She doesn't do research, that's how."

As Tracey was talking, she was getting angrier and angrier.

While Tracey was speaking, Sydney and Carley stopped laughing. It was starting to sound serious.

Sydney asked, "Who's taking care of the dogs?"

"Christine," said Tracey.

"She can use her cell phone," said Carley.

"She can't. They took her purse, her phone, and her car keys. She's stuck there."

Carley asked, "Why didn't she call Granny Nanny?"

"She did, but no one answered. You know she takes the phone off the hook when she's sleeping. She should be up now."

Sydney turned to Carley, "Let's go to my house and make a plan."

Carley said, "Mom, we're going to Sydney's.

Tracey nodded in agreement. She thought, *Wait until I tell Mama about this. She's going to be happy she lives in Florida.*

"Come on, Briggs. We're going back to my house."

Briggs stopped playing with the dogs and asked, "Is Landon going to your house?"

"I don't know. We'll see. I'm going to call Christine and see if he can come over to play."

Sydney, Carley, Briggs, Jazz, and Gypsy walked to Sydney's house. Briggs asked, "Can I stay outside and play with Jazz and Gypsy?"

Sydney looked around and said, "No, Briggs. There's a mean boy going around hurting dogs. Gypsy and Jazz have to come inside."

"What does the mean boy do?" Briggs asked.

"He shoots them with tranquilizer darts, for one thing," said Carley. He shot Gypsy last night. It's a good thing we were outside, or he would have stolen her."

"Wow!" Briggs said. "Poor Gypsy."

"We can't let her out by herself until we catch the boy that's stealing dogs," Carley explained.

"She can come out with me. I'll watch her. I won't let anybody steal Gypsy or Jazz."

"That's sweet of you, Briggs. But we can't be too careful. He would shoot you with a dart just for the fun of it. He's hateful and crazy," Sydney stated.

They were walking to Sydney's house as they were talking. Once they entered the house Briggs said, "I'll just play with them in here until Landon comes over."

"That's a good idea," said Sydney. "If you want something to drink or eat, just let me know. I'll see if Landon can come over."

"Thanks," Briggs said with a smile.

Carley and Sydney went back into the craft room to devise a new plan. While they were making their plans, Christine called Carley's phone.

"Carley, can you watch Landon today. I'll pay you. Mom went to a retreat for a few days, and Landon is getting on my nerves."

"Sure," said Carley. "I'll get Cole to pick him up. We might be going on a little road trip."

Christine was too tired to even ask where they were going. Frankly, she didn't care.

Carley told Sydney, "Christine doesn't know Aunt Crystal is in an insane asylum. She thinks she went to a retreat for a few days."

"Well, I'm not telling her," said Sydney. Once the smallest detail was worked out, Carley said, "I think we can do this."

"Piece of cake," agreed Sydney.

They made a perfect plan to get Aunt Crystal out of the insane asylum.

CHAPTER 9

C arley called Cole. "You can come over now to pick us up. We're at Sydney's."

"It's about time," said Cole. "You told me we were leaving early. It's almost eleven o'clock. Ted probably isn't even home now. I think we are just wasting time and gas."

"The plan's changed. We'll tell you about it when you get here."

While Carley was speaking with Cole, Sydney was changing her outfit. Stacy wore white uniforms to clean houses, because of the cleaners she used. Sydney put on one of her mom's brand-new uniforms and even took her mom's white skirt. She thought, *I'm going to be in so much trouble. Maybe I can wash it before Mom comes home, and she won't notice. Aunt Crystal will make it good when we get her out of the loony house.*

When Sydney came out of her mom's bedroom, she asked, "How do I look?"

Carley stated, "Wow, Sydney! You look like your mom. Even the shoes."

"Yeah," said Sydney. "This is the best part about being the same size as your mom. It's awesome when I wear her designer jeans."

Sydney lifted the skirt to show Carley that she had rolled up pants on under the skirt.

"Now, I'm ready for anything."

"Carley asked, "Why don't you just wear the pants. That's what your mom wears. She doesn't wear skirts to work."

"Because I want to make sure I'm dressed for the part," she explained.

Carley replied, "Well, you are dressed for the part alright."

Carley walked across the two yards to put Gypsy in her house.

Sydney said, "Come on, Briggs. Let's go. We're going to pick up Landon."

Briggs said, "Oh, boy." He rushed outside and waited on the front porch for Sydney.

Sydney made sure Jazz was secured inside. Usually, when no one was home they opened up a garage door so Jazz could go in and out of the garage. Because of all the missing dogs, it was best for her to stay inside.

Cole stopped in front of Sydney's house to pick up Sydney.

"Hi, Briggs," Cole said. "How you doing, buddy?"

"I'm doing great. I love road trips."

Then he went to Carley's house. As Carley was getting into the Explorer, she said, "We need to stop by Aunt Crystal's to pick up Landon."

"That's fine with me," replied Cole. "As long as you know you pay for gas and food."

Carley fussed, "Is that all you think about, Cole? Can't you do something just to be a nice guy?"

Cole answered, "Yes, and no."

Both Sydney and Carley rolled their eyes, but remained quiet. They didn't say anything until they reached Crystal's house. Landon ran to the Explorer as soon as they pulled up. He hopped into the very back seat with Briggs.

"Hi, Briggs," he said.

"Hey, Landon," Briggs said, "What you been doing?"

Landon reached in his pocket and pulled out a handful of joke cards. Within seconds they were deeply engrossed in the cards and laughing at the jokes.

While they were still parked in Crystal's driveway, Sydney reached over and said to Cole, "I have the address already set. Just listen to the GPS."

Carley stated, "Wow, Sydney! You look just like your mom.

"Where are we going," asked Cole.

"Harmony Acres," said Sydney.

The GPS told them to take a right on Kraft Lane, then turn left on Kraft Road. As the GPS was telling directions, Cole asked, "Where's Harmony Acres?"

"It's in Mandeville," Carley answered.

"Mandeville. I thought the dude lived in Loranger."

"Well, we have to take a short detour and pick up Aunt Crystal at Harmony Acres."

"Excuse me, but Mandeville isn't a short detour. It's totally in the wrong direction," stated Cole.

"I know, but if we get her out of Harmony Acres, she'll be so grateful she'll give us all some money. Payday for everybody," smiled Sydney.

Briggs and Landon stopped playing with the cards to listen to their conversation.

Briggs said, "Me, too."

"Me, too," mimicked Landon.

"I hope so," said Sydney. "We'll see. First our plan has to work."

"What's the plan?" Cole asked, while following the GPS directions.

On the way to Harmony Acres, Carley and Sydney filled them all in on the plan.

"If we all work together, this is going to work," Sydney said with a grin.

"Yeah, man," said Briggs.

"You betcha," Landon said.

Cole stated, "In my opinion, we are all going to jail."

While riding to Harmony Acres, Landon told Briggs, "My Maw Maw is always doing crazy things. She even poisoned herself."

Briggs opened his eyes wide and asked, "Poisoned herself, why?"

"It was an accident," stated Landon. She didn't mean to. She ate a poison berry. She thought it was a blackberry."

"What kind of berry?" asked Briggs.

"It was from, um, Sydney, what kind of berry did Maw Maw eat?"

"It was from a Lantana bush," answered Sydney.

Landon looked at Briggs, "It was from a Lantana bush. She thought it was a blackberry bush. Maw Maw got real sick. She called. Landon thought for a second, leaned over and yelled, "Hey Sydney, who did Maw Maw call?"

Sydney answered, "She called Poison Control."

Landon turned towards Briggs and said, "She called Poison Control."

"Wow," said Briggs. What they do?"

"They told her to go to the hospital, or she would die."

"She went to the hospital?" asked Briggs.

"No. She told them she wasn't going to the hospital."

"Well, she's not dead. What happened?" asked Briggs.

Landon answered, "They told her to drink a gallon of milk because she wouldn't go to the hospital."

"Wow!" That's a lot of milk," stated Briggs.

"Yep, that's my Maw Maw."

Landon reached for the joke cards, "Here, let's read some more jokes."

Briggs laughed, "Yeah, I like your joke cards."

Landon and Briggs were once again absorbed in the cards.

Shortly thereafter, they were driving down Harmony Acres' driveway. Harmony Acres were true to its name. Flowers, bushes, trees, and shrubs lined the long drive. The front of the huge, brick building was painted white with black shutters. One large glass door was the entrance. You could see the seven-foot wooden face enclosed the spacious backyard. All in all, it looked very peaceful and appealing.

"This is a nice place," said Cole. "Why does she want to leave?"

"I don't know," said Carley. "She told my mom that it was awful. She said a lot of crazy people live here, and she wants out. So, we are going to get her out."

Cole backed up into the parking space in front of the building beside the handicap parking space.

Sydney looked at Carley. Carley gave her an "I'm not so sure" look.

Carley hesitated. "Maybe this isn't a good idea."

"You can do it, Carley!" encouraged Briggs.

"Yeah, you can do it. Go rescue my Maw Maw," laughed Landon.

"Yeah," laughed Briggs. "Go rescue Landon's Maw Maw."

Carley and Sydney got out of the car, shut the doors, and went to the door of Harmony Acres.

"Now or never," Sydney said to Carley, as she reached for the door into the huge building.

CHAPTER 10

I n a soft whisper, Sydney said, "I'll peek in first and see what the place looks like." Sydney cautiously peeked in the waiting area. It was really small. Only four chairs took up the area. One receptionist on the left was sitting behind an enclosed plexiglass window. The window had a small area opened for her to speak, and a wide ledge for her to hand out and receive information.

The receptionist did not see them. She was laughing at something on her phone.

They were swiftly brushed aside when a man yanked the door opened, stomped inside, and went to the receptionist window.

The man demanded, "You bring me my wife immediately! I'm getting her out of here!"

He hit the ledge of the window — hard.

Sydney said to Carley, "Show time."

She took Carley's left arm and led Carley into the waiting area.

The man was still yelling at the receptionist. He was using language that should not be printed.

Sydney, still holding Carley's left arm, hit the emergency door opener. Sydney was actually surprised when the door opened. Sydney and Carley walked through.

A nurse was talking to a patient. "We have to bring you to your room now, dear. You need your meds."

Groggily, the patient said, "I don't want medicines. They make me sick. I don't want to go to my room. I want to go home."

Carley, in a soft voice said, "My shoe is off. Is my shoe off?"

"No dear," said Sydney. It's all right. We are going to your room now. You need to rest."

"I don't want to," said Carley.

They reached the second set of doors. Sydney, once again, hit the emergency door opener. She was shocked when once again the door opened.

This stage of the building had rooms. Sydney was scanning the names on the room doors. At the same time, she was talking to Carley. She said, "We are almost to your room, dear."

Carley said, "I can't see. Am I wearing my sunglasses?"

"No, dear," said Sydney. You have your eyes shut."

Carley declared, "I can see. You are a genius."

A nurse past them running toward the front of the building.

They came to another set of doors. Holding her breath and saying a silent prayer to herself Sydney hit the emergency door opener, and the doors opened.

"No, dear," said Sydney. You have your eyes shut."

CHAPTER 11

BACK AT THE CAR

Landon and Briggs were still sitting in the back seat of the Explorer. The two seats in the middle were vacant.

Landon got up to talk to Cole. "Cole, how long are we going….."

He didn't complete the sentence. At that moment, two police cars with their sirens on were coming up the drive.

Cole yelled, "Get down. Get down. Don't let them see you."

Landon sat on the floor with his hands wrapped around his knees and tilted over onto his side. Briggs squished down in his seat as far as he could.

Cole said, "Never mind. Get up. Get up. If they see two kids in the car, they'll think we are just waiting for someone."

Briggs sat up straight in the back seat. Landon sat in the seat directly behind the Cole.

Each patrol car held one officer. The officers came out of their cars and entered the building.

"Great!" Cole said.

He turned and looked at Landon, and then Briggs.

Cole stated, "If those two police officers come out with Sydney and Carley, we are out of here."

"You gonna leave them?" Landon asked.

"Yes," said Cole. "If they put them in the back of the police cars, then they are going to jail."

"What about my Maw Maw?" Landon asked.

"I guess she'll have to stay in here forever," said Cole.

"Wow," said Briggs. "That's a really long time."

"Oh, man," said Cole. "I wonder if she got my birthday present yet."

CHAPTER 12

BACK IN THE BUILDING

Sydney still held Carley's arm. This part of the building had some rooms, and a large, open area. A couple of men were sitting in chairs. One of them was talking to himself. The other man was in a daze. Someone was lying on a sofa in the back. A woman with short blonde hair was sitting in a chair by the sofa. One black man and one white man were sitting at a table playing checkers.

A white man with red hair was arguing with a nurse. He looked like he was somewhere in his fifties. He yelled, "I'm hungry! I want to eat! You are starving me!"

"Mr. Ned. I promise you. You had your lunch. Let's go into your room."

"I don't want to go into my room. I'm getting out of here!"

He started to move toward the exit.

The nurse pressed a button on her collar and requested help with an irate patient.

Two huge men wearing all black uniforms went up to the nurse and the man. One man grabbed him while the other one jabbed him with a needle. In the next moment, Ned fell to the floor. One man grabbed his feet, and the other man grabbed him by the shoulders. They picked him up and started toward a room. The nurse following behind.

"We are going to be in so much trouble," whispered Carley.

Sydney whispered, "Shhh."

Sydney kept on walking and looking at the names on the doors. She couldn't see Aunt Crystal's name.

She whispered to Carley, "We are going to have to go to the other side. She's not on this side."

They started toward the opposite side of the room. Out of the corner of Carley's eye, she noticed a movement on the sofa. The person on the sofa had the same red-colored hair as her Aunt Crystal.

Carley whispered to Sydney, "Look on the sofa. That isn't Aunt Crystal, is it?"

Sydney looked. "I don't know. Let's go see, but don't go to fast. We don't want anyone to notice us."

Slowly, they ambled to the sofa. Carley gasped and Sydney almost started to cry. The figure on the sofa didn't look like Aunt Crystal, but it was Aunt Crystal. She had a swollen face, swollen lips, and two black eyes. A large bruise covered her entire forehead.

Sydney slowly looked around and still didn't see a nurse in the area. She bent down and touched Crystal's arm. Crystal moaned.

The lady with the short hair looked straight ahead as she said, "She was fighting with them. You have to be good in here or they will punch you on the forehead and shoot you with drugs. I only have a month left to be here. They'll let me out when my insurance expires."

As the lady spoke to them, Carley and Sydney were trying to get Crystal to sit up.

Sydney whispered, "Aunt Crystal, we are here to get you out. Do you understand?"

Crystal looked confused as she softly said, "Sydney, what happened? Where am I?"

Carley whispered, "You are in an evil place, Aunt Crystal. Can you stand? We have to get you out of here before the nurses come back. Please try to stand up."

Crystal said, "My head hurts. My eyes hurt, too. I don't feel good. I'm so tired."

The lady in the chair said, "Honey, they drugged you. You have to fight it."

"Hu-huh," said Crystal.

Carley and Sydney got on each side of Crystal and helped her to stand.

Sydney pleaded, "Just walk, Aunt Crystal. We'll guide you. Just stay up on your feet. You have to do it. Remember what they did to you. Get mad. Get real mad. When we get you out of here, you can deal with them."

Just before they reached the emergency door opener, a nurse was heading their way. "Where are you goi…"

She stopped speaking when suddenly a terrifying yell came from the short-haired lady sitting in the chair. "Help! Help! Spiders are everywhere!"

The lady jumped up and started to slap at her clothes.

The nurse that had been heading toward them detoured to the screaming lady.

Sydney said a silent thank you to the lady as she pushed the emergency door opener.

They were in the second part of the hospital. Sydney risked glancing around and saw two nurses. They were talking loudly about police officers in the receptionist area.

Sydney thought, *Oh, great! We are going to jail and poor Aunt Crystal is going to have to stay in this horrible place.*

Moments before they reached the next set of doors, a door opened to the left of them. A middle-aged man wearing nothing at all came out of the room. He walked up to Sydney and asked, "Nurse, do you know what happened to my socks? I can't find them."

Sydney pinched her lips together to keep from squealing,

kept her head straight, and said, "Yes, dear. They are under your bed."

The man said, "Thanks." He went back into his room.

Carley wanted to laugh but didn't. She was shaking with fear. She didn't know how much longer she could help hold up their Aunt Crystal.

With a shaking hand, Sydney punched the emergency door opener. They were in the second part of the building. The next set of doors would lead them to the lobby. They were saying silent prayers. So far, they were lucky. Crystal was able to walk. Her head was down and they were practically carrying her, but she was walking.

They didn't see anyone in this section of the building. They were hearing a lot of noise and yelling. But the noise wasn't coming from this section of the building.

They reached the last set of doors. This set of doors led them to the lobby.

Sydney held her breath. Carley was now using both hands to hold one of Crystal's arms. Sydney was holding the other arm. She pushed the emergency door opener.

They walked into the lobby. The scene before them was scary. Two police officers were trying to calm an irate man. The man was telling them what they were doing to his wife. He wanted them to look for themselves and talk with his wife. The administrator insisted that they were not allowed to see the woman.

"Yeah," said the man. They don't want you to see what they did..."

They missed the last of the sentence, as they exited the building. Cole saw them. He rushed to help get Crystal into the car.

"What happened?" he asked.

"Hurry up! Get us out of here," said Carley.

Carley and Sydney managed to get Crystal to the very back sit. "Here, sit by Briggs," said Sydney.

Briggs was too scared to say anything. He didn't even know this lady. He thought, *this lady must have been in a bad accident.*

"Put your seat belt on, Briggs," said Sydney. "Carley, help me with Aunt Crystal's seatbelt." They tried to get Crystal's seat belt latched. They weren't able to because Crystal was leaning every which way.

"We have to get out of here," said Carley.

Sydney and Carley gave up on the seatbelt. Carley got into the passenger seat next to Cole.

Sydney got into the seat behind Carley. Landon was sitting behind the driver's seat. Poor Briggs. He was sitting in the back with Crystal.

Cole made sure everybody but Crystal had on their seatbelts. He certainly didn't want to be pulled over by the police for something like a seat belt violation. He started driving down the lane.

"Now," said Carley. "We will take Aunt Crystal home. After that, we'll go find Ted Brandson."

"No, we won't," said Cole. "We'll have to do it in the morning."

Carley insisted, "If he's the one stealing the dogs, this is the perfect time to watch his house. He gets the dogs early in the morning, or just before dark. He's probably home now."

"That's right," agreed Sydney. "He tried to get Gypsy way after dark yesterday. He's probably sleeping now."

While Sydney, Cole and Carley were discussing the best way to track Ted Brandson, Briggs was watching Crystal. He moved as close to the window as his seatbelt would allow.

Crystal was sleeping soundly one minute. The next minute her eyes would open.

"Where am I?" she would ask.

One time she opened her eyes and stared at Briggs. "Who are you?" she asked.

Briggs didn't answer. He tried squeezing closer to the window. He finally got the nerve to move forward in his seat and whispered to Landon, "Landon, trade places. You have to sit by your Maw Maw. She needs you."

Landon said, "No. She might hit me."

"Why," asked Briggs.

"Because she tells me she's going to knock me out," said Landon.

"But she's your grandmother. It's okay for her to knock you out. It's not okay for her to knock me out."

"She won't knock you out. She don't know you," insisted Landon.

Once again Crystal opened her eyes, looked at Briggs and said, "Oooooh, I think I'm going to be sick."

In less than a second, Briggs unlatched his seatbelt and sat on the floor between Landon and Sydney.

Sydney said, "Briggs, you have to have your seatbelt latched."

Briggs stood his ground. "I'm not going back there. She's going to knock me out and throw up on me. You sit back there. I'm not."

Sydney unlatched her seatbelt and said, "My my, Briggs. I can't believe you are scared of a little old lady—and you go hunting with your dad. Here, you can have my seat and I'll sit by Crystal. Would that make you happy?"

Briggs grinned. "Sure."

Briggs took the seat Sydney had been in, and Sydney sat by Crystal.

Crystal, stretched out on the seat, opened her eyes as Sydney was latching her seatbelt and said, "When did you get here?"

Sydney patted her foot and said, "It's going to be okay, Aunt Crystal. I'll let you know when we are at your house."

Sydney said, "I think I'm with Cole. We should look for Ted Branson early tomorrow morning. Let's get to his house before daylight. This has been a bad day. We need some sleep. We know where he lives. When we see him, we can follow him. He might lead us to the dogs if he's the dog thief."

"I guess so," said Carley. "I'm tired. By the time we get Crystal home, it'll be late. We still have to let Gypsy and Jazz out."

So, it was agreed. Start fresh the next day.

But sometimes things happen unexpectedly.

CHAPTER 13

Things went smoothly for the rest of the ride home. Occasionally, Crystal would open her eyes and say some really bad words about what she was going to do to the man who knocked her out with his fist.

When she did this, Sydney just patted her on her foot and said, "We are almost home, Aunt Crystal. It'll be okay."

Briggs was still sitting in the seat behind Carley, and did not say a word. He tried to make himself invisible. He didn't want Crystal to do to him what she was planning to do to the people at Harmony Acres.

Landon sat in his seat behind Cole. Every now and then he would turn sideways and glance at his Maw Maw. He made sure he was quiet. He didn't want a bop on his head.

Every couple of minutes Crystal looked at Sydney and gave her an order: "I need you to give Rosco his medicine."

"Okay," said Sydney.

"Don't forget to clean the kennels."

"Okay."

"I need you to feed the dogs. Don't forget to put ice in their water bowls."

"Okay," Aunt Crystal.

That went on and on. Sydney thought, *I want to go home. This has been a wretched day.*

Finally, Cole pulled into the turning lane on Kraft Road. One more minute and they would be at Aunt Crystal's house.

Carley yelled, "Turn around! There's the truck. I know it's the one. Get behind it so we can see the license plate!"

Cole turned onto Kraft Road, backed onto the highway, and speeded to catch up with the old white truck.

Crystal yelled, "Are we home yet?"

Sydney replied, "Not yet, Aunt Crystal. It'll be a couple more minutes."

Carley yelled, "Don't lose him! Whatever you do, don't lose him!"

Cole was still speeding to catch up to the truck. Within moments, the truck was on the interstate, heading towards Loranger. Cole got real close to the truck and yelled to Carley, "Write down the license plate number."

Carley said, "I don't have paper and pencil."

Cole said, "I have a pen in my glove compartment. Get it out!"

Carley opened the glove compartment, emptied most of its contents, found the pen, and wrote the license plate number on her hand.

Sydney said to Cole, "Get back. We don't want him to think we are following him."

Cole said, "You and Carley are getting on my nerves."

"Well, we have his license plate number now. We can back up some," explained Sydney.

Cole eased back on the gas pedal. He allowed one truck and one car to get in front of him. He was still following the old white truck.

Cole said, "Carley, is that the right number?"

"It looks like it's the same. I'm not sure. I don't have the paper with me, with his license number."

Crystal yelled, "Where am I?"

"You are on your way home," said Sydney.

Sydney patted her foot again.

"I had a dream," said Crystal. "A man beat me up and I squashed him like a bug."

"That's nice," said Sydney. "What's the number of the plate, Carley?"

Carley looked at her hand and read off the number.

Sydney yelled, "That's the number the man gave us. I know it is. I left my notebook at home, but I'm sure it's the number. Don't lose him, Cole."

Crystal asked, "What did you lose, Sydney? When are we going to get home?"

"Everything is fine," Sydney told Crystal.

"I got this," said Cole.

Crystal went to sleep again.

Landon and Briggs kept their eyes on the truck ahead.

Landon said, "Don't lose him, Cole."

Briggs said, "Yeah, Cole. Don't lose him. This is fun, huh, Landon?"

Landon replied, "Yeah. We're going to get that old dog thief."

"We sure are," Briggs excitedly said.

Crystal woke up and said, "You getting the idiot that knocked me out?"

Sydney humored her and said, "Yeah."

Crystal said, "When you get him, give him to me. I'm gonna … [more bad language]."

The truck turned left onto a small blacktop road. Cole continued to keep his distance while following the truck.

Shortly thereafter, the old white truck turned right onto a narrow gravel drive. Trees, vines, and bushes lined both sides of the drive. The ditch was blocked, full of tall weeds and grass.

Cole started to follow the truck, but Carley stopped him.

"Don't go down that drive, Cole."

"Why?" asked Cole. "You told me to follow him."

"I know," explained Carley. "But this drive might lead to a dead end and we'll be trapped."

"What do we do then?" Cole asked.

"I don't know," answered Carley.

"Leave me alone. I want to sleep," moaned Crystal.

"Okay," said Sydney. She patted Crystal's foot again. Crystal went back to sleep.

"One of us can get out and follow him," said Carley.

"Who?" Sydney asked.

Carley and Cole looked at Sydney. Briggs and Landon looked at Sydney.

Sydney looked at Cole; then she looked at Carley.

Cole and Carley continued to stare at Sydney.

Cole finally said, "Sydney, you are the smallest. You can walk along the edge of the drive and not be seen. If you see someone, you can hide behind one of the trees."

"I'm not the smallest," said Sydney. "Briggs is the smallest."

Briggs opened his eyes wide and declared, "Not me!"

Sydney argued, "I'm dressed in white. They'll see me. I'll need to be camouflaged. Cole, take your shirt off. It's brown and it'll blend with the trees."

Cole took off his brown shirt and handed it to Sydney. She put the brown shirt on over her white uniform top. She rolled her pants legs down and took off her skirt. The pants were white. She made a disapproval face and looked at Cole.

"Don't look at me," said Cole. "I'm not giving you my pants. I'll look crazy driving in nothing but a T-shirt and underwear. No way. Not happening."

"I wasn't going to ask you to take off your pants," declared Sydney. "They are so big I wouldn't be able to walk if I wore them. So be quiet and stop complaining."

Sydney made sure her cell phone was on silent and put it in her pants pocket.

She looked at Carley and said, "I'll call you if something goes wrong."

"Okay. Be careful," Carley said.

Sydney started walking down the driveway, staying as close to the tree line as possible.

Cole backed the Explorer into the drive and pulled out again so that he was facing toward the way he came.

As Cole was maneuvering the Explorer into position, Crystal sat up, opened her eyes, and said, "What are you doing? Where are we? What happened?"

She looked at Landon. "What are you doing, Landon?" She looked at Briggs. "Who are you?"

Briggs squealed, "Ugh, I want to go with Sydney. She needs my help."

Quickly, he zoomed out the side door and started running down the drive toward Sydney.

Landon said, "I'm going with Briggs. Sydney needs my help, too."

He zoomed out the side door and ran down the drive toward Sydney.

Cole and Carley jumped out of the Explorer and ran after Briggs and Landon.

"Come back," hollered Carley.

Briggs made it to Sydney. Landon jogged to the other side of Briggs.

"I'm going with you, Sydney. You need my help," insisted Briggs.

"Me too," said Landon.

"You can't come with me. I have to sneak up on Ted and see what he's up to without him seeing me. He'll see three people."

"But I don't want to be by that crazy lady. She's going to rip my face off."

"No, she isn't, Briggs. She's always going to rip off somebody's face. She never does. She tells me that all the time. See, I still have my face."

By that time Carley and Cole made it to them.

Landon said, "Briggs, my Maw Maw isn't really mean. Just sometimes."

Sydney pleaded, "Please, Briggs, this is really important. We have to see if Ted is the one stealing the dogs. If somebody stole your dog, wouldn't you want someone to find the thief?"

Landon asked, "If Delcha was missing, would you find her?"

"We'd sure try," said Carley. "That's what we do."

"Okay," said Briggs.

Carley, Cole, Landon, and Briggs started back to the Ford Explorer. When they got there, Crystal had moved from the back seat to the seat behind the passenger seat. To get into the middle seat behind the driver's seat, you had to get past Crystal. Briggs peeped into the Explorer. He got into the front passenger seat.

Carley stated, "That's my seat, Briggs."

Briggs folded his arms across his chest and said, "I'm not moving."

Carley made a huffing sound, rolled her eyes, crossed over Crystal, and sat in the seat behind Cole.

Poor Landon. He looked around, and the only vacant seat was the double seat in the back. He huffed and puffed as he got into the back seat. He folded his arms across his chest and said nothing at all.

Quickly, he zoomed out the side door and started running down the drive toward Sydney.

CHAPTER 14

Sydney very slowly and carefully continued to walk along the drive. She was ready to get behind one of the many large pine trees if necessary.

She went around a sharp bend in the driveway and saw a huge, faded old barn. It looked as though it might have been red at one time, but now it was hard to tell.

Trees and shrubs surrounded the barn. She looked around for a house but didn't see one. Very slowly, she inched a little closer toward the barn. She noticed a narrow dirt path that was just wide enough for a car or truck to go down. It seemed to be used often. She followed the path and was surprised when the path opened up to a large parking area. The parking area was packed with gravel. Weeds were growing in the gravel, so she knew the parking lot hadn't been in recent use.

She continued looking around the parking area and that's when she saw it—the old white pick-up truck. In front of the pick-up truck was a brown Nissan Maxima. She immediately hid behind a tree and waited.

Sydney pulled out her phone to check the time. It was five-thirty. She thought, *Man, it's going to be dark soon. I won't be able to use my phone flashlight; they'll see it. I'm calling Carley.*

She scrolled through her contacts until she saw Carley's number. She hit the call button and quickly discovered she had no service. Sydney couldn't get in touch with Carley. *Now what?* She thought.

At that moment she saw a movement at the barn. She knelt down behind a big pine tree. Two people came out through the back door. One of them was a boy with nasty, greasy, shoulder-length brown hair. The other was a fat man with grey hair. He wore a grey suit. He looked disgustingly evil, and Sydney immediately disliked him.

The boy and the man spoke for a few minutes. The fat man got into the brown Nissan Maxima and drove down the path, passing Sydney.

Sydney hoped the man wouldn't see her behind the tree. He didn't.

Sydney, very slowly and carefully
continued to walk along the drive.

CHAPTER 15

BACK AT THE FORD EXPLORER

"How long has Sydney been gone?" Briggs asked.

That was the fifth time he had asked the same question.

"You think she's okay?" Briggs asked.

That was the fifth time he had asked that question.

Cole said, "She's been gone forty-five minutes, Briggs."

Landon said, "She needs to hurry. I'm hungry and thirsty. I want to go home now."

Briggs said, "I'm hungry and thirsty, too. Call Sydney and tell her to come back."

Cole got out of the Explorer and said, "I don't have food, but I have water. I'll get us some. It's in the back."

He went to the back of the Explorer, opened the back door, and passed bottles of water to Landon. Landon's job was to pass the water to Briggs, Carley, and his Maw Maw.

Cole heard a car coming down the drive. He threw the bottles that were in his hand onto the back seat, abruptly shutting the back doors of the Explorer.

As he was rushing to get into the driver's seat, the brown Nissan Maxima pulled out of the driveway.

The old man driving the car stopped alongside of the Explorer, opened his window, and asked Cole, "What are you doing?"

Cole opened his mouth to say something, but suddenly he was rendered speechless. His mouth wouldn't work; his brain froze.

Carley jumped out of the Explorer, quickly coming up with an explanation. "Sir, we are trying to locate Lana's Lane. Can you help us?"

"I never heard of it, and I've been here for years," the old man said.

"Oh man," said Carley. "We don't know what to do. We are trying to take my aunt home. She had surgery. She was giving us directions and fell asleep. I think the directions she gave us are wrong."

The old man raised his right eyebrow and said, "She's your aunt and you don't know where she lives?"

"That's right," said Carley. "We've never been to her house. She comes to our house."

"Then why did you pick her up?" he asked.

"Because my mom couldn't. She asked Cole to do it. That's Cole." She pointed to Cole.

All Cole could do was nod his head up and down like a bobblehead.

"Well, if you know what's good for you, leave. This is privately owned."

He stayed there waiting for them to start moving.

Carley said, "I'll call my mom. Maybe she can tell us where we need to go." She reached for her phone.

The man looked out his window and laughed. It wasn't a funny laugh; it was more of an evil laugh.

"Call her," he laughed.

Carley took her phone out of her pocket and tried to call Sydney. NO SERVICE showed up on her display screen.

"I don't have any service," said Carley.

"Of course you don't," said the evil fat man. "This whole place is blocked from all electronic devices. We don't have cell or internet. We don't even have a landline telephone.

"You won't get service until you are at least 50 yards off this road." The evil man spoke in a loud and menacing voice. "So get!"

With shaking hands, Cole turned the key in the ignition and started the engine. Carley got back in the Explorer, shut the door, and was heading to her seat just as Cole slammed down on the gas pedal. Carley lost her balance and landed on her Aunt Crystal. The bottled waters fell off the back seat and were rolling all over the floor.

All the commotion woke up Crystal. At least she woke up much more alert than she had been since leaving Harmony Acres. The drugs seemed to be wearing off.

"What's going on here?" she insisted.

Carley was on the floor. Cole was speeding down the road to get away as fast as he safely could.

The evil fat man followed them to make sure they were really leaving. Cole pulled into the first service station he saw and stopped. He couldn't keep his hands and body from shaking.

Once Cole stopped at the service station, the big evil man drove on.

Crystal yelled, "Somebody better tell me what's going on here."

Carley was still on the floor. She was upset over leaving Sydney. Therefore, she yelled back at her Aunt Crystal, "We got you out of the mental institution. If it wasn't for us, you would still be there. They beat you, and drugged you all up. Can't you remember?"

Crystal saw the bottles of water, grabbed one and said, "I have to flush this medicine out of my system." She tilted the bottle of water to her mouth and drank it all without stopping. Not once.

She said, "I have to use the restroom."

As she was getting out of the Explorer, Briggs said, "I have to go too."

Landon chimed in, "I do too. I can't hold it anymore."

"We'll all go," said Carley.

They all exited the vehicle and marched into the service station.

He went to the back of the Explorer, opened the back door, and was passing bottles of water to Landon.

CHAPTER 16

BACK AT THE BARN

Sydney saw the brown Nissan Maxima pull out of the dirt path and onto the gravel driveway. She continued watching the barn to see any signs of anyone else other than the driver of the white truck. She thought, *I need to look in the window. I can't stay here all night. I need to risk it.*

Slowly, she inched her way to the nearest window, stood on tippy toes, and peered into the window.

What she saw made her sick. There must have been fifty dogs in kennels. All the water and food dishes were empty. The dogs looked depressed.

They didn't even bark when the greasy-haired boy entered with a roll cart carrying food and water. She ducked back down. She didn't want to risk him seeing her.

Slowly, she inched her head high enough to see what he was doing. He was taking the empty dishes out and putting in fresh food and water.

She was so engrossed in what she was seeing that she didn't notice someone walking in her direction until her hair was grabbed and yanked, forcing her head backward. She couldn't see her attacker. All she knew was the attacker was mighty strong. *An ugly monster has me,* she thought.

As he pulled her by her hair into the barn, he said, "Look what I found outside spying on us.

That was when Sydney was able to see the person who grabbed her. It was a real ugly man.

She thought, *Yes, I was right. He is an ugly monster.* He was huge, with black hair, and squished-up, beady-looking eyes. Ugly monster was too nice of a term to describe him.

"What are you going to do with her?" asked the greasy-haired boy.

He went to reach for her hair again and she kicked him as hard as she could on his kneecap. He went down a little but was still able to yank her hair. He pulled her into one of the large kennels and latched the door.

He told the greasy-haired boy, "Watch that she doesn't get out; I have to get a lock."

While the ugly monster man went in search of a lock, Sydney asked, "Why are you stealing people's dogs?"

Since the moment Sydney entered the barn, the dogs had barked continuously. The greasy- haired boy yelled over the barking dogs, "For money, stupid."

"You're the stupid one. Making money stealing dogs. You are going to go to jail. Why steal people's dogs?"

"These dogs are here to train the pit bulls that we steal, stupid girl," he said.

"Hahahaha," he started laughing.

"You're the stupid one. That doesn't make sense. How can they help train pit bulls?"

He pointed to a doorway. "You see that door. That door leads to the pit bulls. We train them to fight. First, we don't feed them. We have to make sure they are really hungry. Then, we put them in another section we call the arena. The pit bulls are taught to kill. We start off with the smallest dogs first. We work up to the largest dogs. After they kill, then, we teach them to fight. We feed them a lot, give them shots to make them strong, and mean. Then, another month from now, we bring the pit bulls to the arena. People from all over the States bring their pit bulls to fight. It's real fun. Too bad you won't be able to see the fights."

"You can't do that. It's against the law," Sydney furiously stated.

He smiled as he said, "So what! We can do whatever we want."

The ugly monster man came back carrying paracord. "I'll tie the door with this. She won't be able to escape."

After tying the door with the paracord, he put the excess paracord on top of the next kennel.

"We can't leave her here forever. Where will we put her?" the greasy-haired boy asked.

"Wherever the boss tells us. Maybe she'll go missing like these dogs here," he wickedly laughed. "But for now, she stays in the kennel. Understood!"

"Understood."

Then, they both went into the room that had the pit bulls.

Sydney didn't know how she was going to get out. *I wish I would have taken one of Granny's survival bracelets when she was passing them out. I think it had a small cutting tool on it. No matter, Cole and the gang know where I am. They'll get help.*

As soon as the men walked into the other room, the dogs quit barking.

The place was well lit so Sydney was able to see most of the dogs.

She gasped when she recognized one. It was Eddie. Eddie Spaghetti was his nickname. He still had on his neckband her granny made special for him. She loudly said, "Eddie Spaghetti, I'm going to get you out of here. I don't know how, but I am."

Eddie knew Sydney well. She always held him close to her after she bathed him. He would love to snuggle. And he loved his neckbands. Everyone would tell him how cute and sweet he looked when he had on a neckband. He knew Sydney. He scratched at the kennel door when he heard her speaking to him.

Sydney continued to scan all the kennels. Eddie wasn't the only dog here that her Aunt Crystal sat. There was Bella, the boxer. Sydney started to cry when she saw another dog Aunt Crystal sat. It was Josie. Whenever Sydney sat down, Josie would climb on her lap. She was a goldendoodle, one of the sweetest dogs ever. Next to Josie was a black labradoodle.

That has to be Laura's dog, thought Sydney.

"Jolie!" Sydney yelled.

The black labradoodle looked at Sydney.

"I'm getting you out of here, Jolie. You too, Josie. I'm getting you all out!" Sydney yelled.

I have to get out of here, and fast.

The greasy-haired boy came back to his cart and continued feeding the dogs. Once his cart was empty, he went back into a room and got some more food and water. Sydney assumed that room must be a kitchen. As he put the food and water into the kennels, he took out the empty bowls. He did that until all the dogs were fed and watered. He totally ignored Sydney. He rolled the cart into the kitchen. Then he went into the door where he said the pit bulls were kept.

A third man Sydney never saw before came out of the pit bulls' room. He was medium height with dark brown hair, and brown eyes. It was noticeable that he spent a lot of time at the gym. His muscles were huge. Sydney was going to name him Mr. Pit Bull but she didn't want to insult the pit bulls of the world. Sydney named him Mr. Big.

Mr. Big was leading a pit bull on a leash. He led the pit bull into the room that the greasy-haired boy called the arena.

Mr. Big then came out of the arena, opened the kennel where Eddie was kept, and took out Eddie.

"Put him back," yelled Sydney. "Leave him alone."

As Mr. Big was heading toward the arena, Sydney stared screaming and crying, "AARRGGH--let him go!"

She screamed as loud as she could. She just kept screaming and crying. There was nothing she could do.

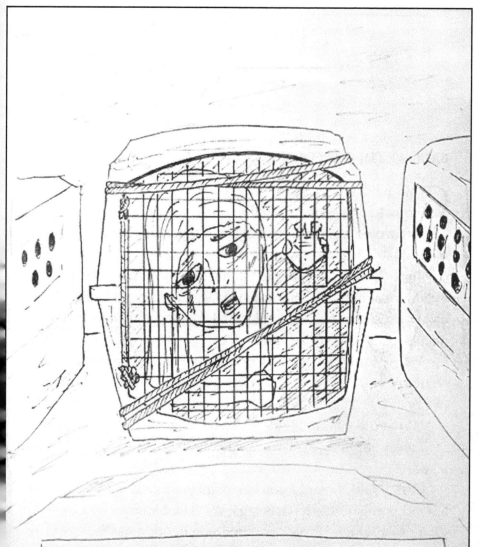

She gasped when she recognized
one. It was Eddie.

CHAPTER 17

BACK AT THE EXPLORER

Cole paid for everyone to get a soft drink and something to eat at the service station, only with the assurance that Crystal would pay him back. Her car, purse, phone, and keys were still at Harmony Acres.

Carley called her mom to tell her they had Aunt Crystal and would be home soon. Her mom, Tracey, said that she had been trying to call but only got voicemail. Carley explained that they were in an area that had no service.

Tracey told Carley that Christine called and said the police went to Crystal's house. They wanted to know the whereabouts of Crystal.

"What did Christine say?" asked Carley.

Tracey replied, "Christine said she hadn't seen her mother all day."

Carley said, "Would you call Aunt Stacy and tell her that we are in Loranger? We have Briggs. We'll be home soon."

Tracey asked, "What are you doing in Loranger?"

"It's a long story. Aunt Crystal will explain when we get home."

They said their goodbyes and hung up.

Crystal wasn't hung over anymore from all the drugs she had been forcibly given at Harmony Acres. She turned around and didn't see Sydney. She asked, "Where's Sydney? I thought she was in the car. Was I dreaming?"

Carley drank a little of her drink. Then she said, "Aunt

Crystal, I'll have to tell you from the beginning before you will understand, but we have to go back to find Sydney. It's a really long story."

Crystal demanded, "Drive, Cole, and give the short version, Carley, and hurry it up."

Carley started to tell the story. "Laura came to my house wanting Sydney and me to find her dog. We went to all her neighbors to see if they lost or knew someone who lost a dog. We told you and you said you would put it on your neighborhood watch. Our investigation led us to a dirty, greasy-haired boy, driving an old white pick-up truck. We had to rescue you from the nut house. On the way to your house we saw the truck. We followed the truck and he went down that gravel driveway. Sydney went down the driveway to see what the greasy-haired boy was doing. We parked so we could leave fast when Sydney came back. It was getting dark. A mean man came by and told us to leave. We had to leave that spot. He was watching us, so we had to drive to the service station. You woke up. You've been sleeping all day. And here we are. We have to find Sydney, fast."

Carley didn't eat any of her chips, and she couldn't drink any more of her drink. She felt sick.

Cole made it to the exact spot he had been before. Once again, he pulled into the driveway, backed up, and pulled forward slightly, so he could make a hasty escape.

Crystal got angry. Very angry was Crystal. This day hadn't gone as planned. She thought she was going to a nice, peaceful resort. She should be getting a massage, manicure, and pedicure. Instead, she wound up in a place she wouldn't take her dogs. And now here. She was ready to take somebody down.

Crystal finished off her Coke. She needed the caffeine. She stomped out of the Explorer.

Carley came out of the Explorer. "It's dark now, Aunt Crystal.

You can't see down this road. We can use my phone's light."

"We can't use the light, Carley. They'll see us coming. You can stay at the car. I can handle this."

"No. I'm going with you. It's my fault she's here."

Crystal said, "Let's go."

Crystal turned to Cole. "Keep an eye on those kids."

"Yes, ma'am," said Cole.

Briggs looked at Landon and whispered, "I think I like your Maw Maw."

"Yeah," said Landon. "She might be crazy, but she's okay."

CHAPTER 18

BACK AT THE BARN

Sydney kept screaming, screeching, yelling, and crying. Only the dogs in the barn could hear her. They yowled.

Eventually she stopped screaming and started to try to untie the paracord. The knots were on the outside of the kennel. She had to try to turn the knots toward her. It was hard because she was on her knees and hunched over. The kennel was not high enough for her to stand. Sydney was making slow progress.

She stopped when she heard a loud scream and cussing come from the arena area. It was a fourth man wearing a padded suit. She had not seen him before now. He stumbled out of the arena into the dogs' room, holding his neck. Blood was oozing from the left side of his neck and a big bite mark was on the man's hand.

Mr. Big and greasy-haired boy weren't far behind.

They were shook up, and walking around in circles. "What do we do? What do we do?" greasy-haired boy said.

"Um, get a rag and put it on his neck to catch the blood," said Mr. Big.

Sydney said, "Let me out. I know what to do."

The greasy-haired boy said, "Tell us."

"No. You have to let me out first. If you don't, I won't tell you. He can bleed to death for all I care."

She crossed her arms.

The greasy-haired boy looked at Mr. Big.

Mr. Big grinned. "You can let her out. I'll put her back in. No problem."

The greasy-haired boy took out his pocket knife, cut the paracord, unlatched the kennels, and freed Sydney.

By this time, the man in the padded suit was lying on the floor, moaning. Blood was still oozing from his neck. Sydney yelled, "Get me a blanket, quick. He's going into shock. We have to keep him warm."

She really didn't know if he was going into shock or not. *What do I know?* She thought. It was something she saw on television. *It sounded good.*

Mr. Big went in search of a blanket.

She turned to the greasy-haired boy. "Get me some material so we can hold it against the wound. Hurry!" *That sort of sounded good too.*

The greasy-haired boy found some rags in the kitchen part of the barn. He handed them to Sydney. She folded them and used one to put pressure on the man's neck. She handed the other one to the greasy-haired boy and told him to put pressure on the man's hand. He did.

Mr. Big was still looking for a blanket.

Sydney asked, "What happened?"

He said, "The pit bull attacked him."

"Well," said Sydney. "That's one smart pit bull."

Mr. Big came back with a blanket and handed it to Sydney.

With one hand, she covered the man. With the other hand she continued to hold pressure on the man's neck. He was still bleeding, but Sydney knew it really wasn't that bad. She wasn't going to tell them that.

"You need to take him to the hospital," she demanded. "It's urgent!"

Mr. Big said, "I can't. I don't have a ride."

He looked at the greasy-haired boy and said, "You have to take him in your truck."

"I don't want to take him. He'll bleed all over my seat."

Mr. Big yelled, "You better take him. If he dies, and Boss knows you wouldn't take him to the hospital, you will be in big trouble."

Reluctantly, the greasy-haired boy said, "I'll take him, but you have to help me clean my truck when I get back."

Mr. Big was so big that he picked up the bleeding man as though he weighed no more than five pounds. He carried him to the truck.

While they were bringing the injured man to the truck, Sydney hurried and grabbed a leash that was hanging on a peg by the door. She went to Jolie's kennel, and released her. Jolie jumped up and down excitedly. She put her paw on Sydney's shoulders and licked Sydney's face. Sydney put the leash on Jolie.

"Good girl, Jolie," said Sydney. "Let's find Eddie."

Sydney walked into the part of the barn that was named the arena. Eddie was sitting on the ground and the pit bull was standing beside him. When Eddie saw Sydney, he ran as fast as his little feet would carry him to her. Sydney scooped him up and held him close to her. The pit bull was smiling as he ran up to Sydney. He was wagging his nub of a tail. He stopped in front of her for a head scratch. As Sydney was scratching his head, she paid attention to his coloring. He was tan and white.

She asked, "Are you Brutus?"

The pit bull's smile widened, and he hopped up and down and turned around. Sydney laughed to see the excitement of the dog. They were all so happy.

The happiness didn't last long. When Sydney turned around to leave, Mr. Big was blocking the door. He was carrying a dart gun.

Sydney still held Jolie's leash and was holding Eddie. Brutus, the pit bull, stood beside Sydney, showed his teeth, and growled.

Sydney stepped in front of Brutus as the man raised a dart gun to shoot the pit bull.

The man yelled, "Step aside, little girl, or I'll shoot you."

He started to raise the dart gun again, but something hit him in the middle of his back. He fell to the floor, dropping the dart gun.

He started to get up, and at the same time tried to turn around. WHAM! He was punched between the eyes, and went down, HARD.

Sydney yelled, "Aunt Crystal, Aunt Crystal. You're back. I'm so happy to see you!"

With Eddie still in her arm, and Jolie still on a leash, she ran to Crystal and gave her a one- armed hug.

Carley also gave her Aunt Crystal a big hug. "I'm so glad we rescued you from the crazy house."

Crystal said, "Sydney, call 911."

"I can't. We don't have service here."

"Then we'll do the next best thing," Crystal said. "We'll tie him up."

Sydney proudly stated, "I know where there's some para-cord. I'll get it."

Sydney ran back into the room with the dogs and retrieved the excess paracord. She brought it to her Aunt Crystal.

Crystal took the paracord and tied the man's hands behind his back, real tight. She tied his feet together. She even had enough paracord to tie it from his hands to his feet.

She stood up, looked at her work and declared, "He won't be going anywhere for a while. Let's get out of here."

Sydney was still carrying Eddie. Carley had taken Jolie's leash. Brutus was walking alongside Carley. Before Sydney left the barn, she hollered, "I'm coming back for all of you, I promise."

Once they got back to the Explorer, Cole, Briggs, and Landon opened the doors for them. All three were talking at the same time, wanting to know what happened.

"First, let's get to a spot where we can call 911," said Crystal.

While Cole was driving back to the service station, Landon and Briggs were in the back of the Explorer, playing with Jolie and Brutus.

Sydney was telling them about the dogs, and how Aunt Crystal knocked out Mr. Big.

Once at the gas station, Cole got out. He asked the clerk exactly where they were so he could call 911. After calling 911, he got back into the Explorer to wait on the responders.

Within fifteen minutes, the responders were at the service station. Crystal got out of the Explorer to speak with the responders.

She told the responder in charge, "You'll have to follow us. It's hard to explain the location of the barn."

Cole jumped out of the Explorer. "We have to hurry," he said. That's the brown Nissan Maxima. He's going to the barn. I know it. He'll let the man loose."

Cole and Crystal raced back to the Explorer. Cole speeded toward the driveway. This time he drove up the driveway. He got out of the Explorer as two men were getting out of the Nissan Maxima. Crystal also got out of the Explorer.

Mr. Evil, the owner of the Nissan, came toward Cole yelling, "What do you think--"

He stopped speaking and his eyes widened as he saw the 911 vehicle. Right behind the 911 vehicle were two police cruisers.

"Wow!" said Briggs. "Landon, I want to hang out with you all the time. This is a great day!"

Landon proudly stated, "This is nothing. You need to be at Maw Maw's house on a busy day."

Briggs opened his eyes even wider. "Wow!"

He started to get up, and at the
same time turn around, and, WHAM!

CHAPTER 19

Crystal, Cole, Sydney, and Carley walked to the police officers. The officers stared at Crystal. One of them asked, "What happened to you?"

"We can get to that later. Right now we have to take care of the dogs. The people here ----"

She stopped midsentence. The owner of the Nissan Maxima, Mr. Evil, walked up to the police officers.

"Hi, Officer," he said. "I'm Brian Hutch. I want these people arrested for trespassing."

"That's the man stealing everyone's dogs," Cole yelled.

"Yeah," said Sydney. He uses them to train pit bulls to fight. He makes them kill the smaller dogs. The boy in the white truck told me. He had to take a man to the hospital. The pit bull attacked him."

"Yeah," Landon hollered from the Explorer's window.

"Yeah," hollered Briggs. "He's the one."

"Where's the pit bull that attacked the man?" one of the officers asked.

Protectively, she put her hand on Brutus. She wasn't about to rat out Brutus.

"He escaped into the woods," Sydney answered.

The officer asked, "Can you describe the pit bull?"

Sydney sounded distraught. "No, I was so upset. The dogs barking, blood everywhere, man on ground screaming, it was just too much."

The other officer called Animal Control to have the dogs in the barn picked up. While they were waiting for Animal Control,

Crystal went into the barn to search the dogs. There were four dogs that belonged to her clients: Bella, Josie, Annie, and Trixie. She rounded them up and brought them to the Explorer.

The officer told Crystal that she was not allowed to take the dogs. Only Animal Control could take them.

She informed him, "These dogs belong to my clients. I will take them with me. If you want, I'll call my clients and you can speak with them about this matter."

She knew she wouldn't be able to call her clients. Her phone was still at Harmony Acres with all her clients' contact numbers.

After taking a good look at her face, he didn't argue.

Briggs and Landon was in the back seat holding Trixie, the schnauzer, and Josie, the goldendoodle. Crystal found leashes in the barn for the two boxers, Bella and Annie. Cole led them to the Explorer. They happily jumped into the Explorer.

Sydney never released Eddie Spaghetti. She continued to hold him. Brutus, the pit bull, never left Sydney's side. He wanted to stay by Eddie. Carley led Jolie to the Explorer. She happily joined the other dogs.

The Explorer was packed.

In total, the Explorer held six people and seven dogs.

When Animal Control got there, Crystal asked them where they were going with the dogs. She wanted to put it on her neighborhood watch and social media.

Once everything was taken care of, they were off to Aunt Crystal's house.

With all the people and dogs, the trip to Crystal's house was anything but boring.

CHAPTER 20

W ithout any more incidents, they managed to get to Crystal's house. By that time, it was eleven o'clock.

Stacy and Tracey met them there.

Dogs and people plowed out of the Explorer. Stacy walked to Briggs. "I talked to your mom, Briggs. Since it's so late, she said you can spend the night if you want. If you don't want, I'll bring you home."

"Can Landon stay the night?"

Stacy smiled. "Sure. "You can have a sleepover."

Stacy asked, "Landon, you want to have a sleep over at my house with Briggs?"

Landon jumped up and down. "Yes! Can I, Mom?"

"I guess so," Christine said.

Christine glanced over at her mom and said, "Oh, no. What happened to you?"

Stacy looked at her and repeated the same question.

"I'll tell you later. We have to get the dogs in the house. Don't leave, Cole, until I come back."

"Okay," said Cole.

This was one time Cole wasn't in a hurry to get home. He was hoping for some money. He said to himself, *I hope she gives me money for all my trouble and expenses.*

It only took a couple of minutes for her to let the dogs into the backyard. She knew they had to use the bathroom and stretch their legs. While the dogs were in the backyard, Crystal went into her expense cabinet. She came back out and handed Sydney, Carley, Landon, and Briggs each a $100 bill. She gave Cole $200.

She smiled, "You get extra for your expenses, and for being an extraordinary chauffeur."

Cole said, "Thanks, Ms. Crystal. I was happy to help."

Sydney and Carley rolled their eyes as they looked at each other.

"Thanks, Maw Maw," said Landon.

"Wow! Thanks, Ms. Crystal," said Briggs. "If you ever need help, just let me know."

Crystal smiled. "When you get older, I'll hire you to help take care of the dogs."

Briggs nodded his head yes and gave her a big grin.

Carley and Sydney also thanked her.

Crystal said, "Don't forget, Sydney. You have to be here at seven o'clock tomorrow morning."

CHAPTER 21

Carley said, "Cole, we have --"

Before Carley could complete the sentence, Cole said, "I know. I know."

Carley was holding Jolie's leash, as she and Sydney walked to Ms. Ann's front door. Carley knocked. No one answered. Carley knocked again.

They heard someone walking across the living room. Behind the door someone yelled, "Who's there?"

Carley said, "Its Carley and Sydney. We have a present for Laura."

Ms. Ann was in the process of opening the door and asking, "Can it wait until tomorrow"

Laura is --"

She stopped speaking when she saw Jolie. She put her hand to her mouth and started crying. She hugged Jolie, Carley, and Sydney. "Come in," she said.

"Laura is going to be so happy. She hardly eats and sleeps. She's been so depressed. She thought you wouldn't find her. She even said you probably wouldn't even try. I was so right when I passed your house and told her a smart girl lives there."

Carley whispered to Sydney, "It was my house she passed."

Sydney gave her a squished up face look.

They made it down the hall to Laura's room. Jolie was so excited, she pulled the leash out of Carley's hand, and jumped onto Laura's bed. She nuzzled Laura under her chin. Then she gave Laura some wet kisses on her cheek. Laura opened her eyes and squealed when she saw Jolie. She wrapped her little arms around Jolie's neck and told her how much she loved her.

"You are my bestest friend. I love you so much."

Sydney and Carley only smiled.

Laura looked up at her grandma and said, "Where did you fi..."

That's when she saw Carley and Sydney. She climbed out of bed to give each one a hug.

"Thank you so much. How much do I owe you? I get an allowance. I'll give you my allowance every week."

Sydney said, "You don't owe us anything. A nice lady paid it for you."

Laura started to cry all over again as she ran to Jolie and gave her hugs and kisses.

Sydney turned to Ms. Ann. "Just to let you know, if you or anyone you know needs a pet sitter, go to Pet Pal Pet Sitting Service. It's on Kraft Lane. She's the best. I would give you her card, but I don't have one. She helped us get Jolie back."

"She sure did," Carley said. "She beat up one of the men that took Jolie. Knocked him out."

"Thanks! I'll keep that in mind. Thank you for everything. Would you like something to drink and eat?"

"No, thank you," Carley said. "If we stay too long our driver will leave us."

Cole didn't leave them. He brought them home with parting words of wisdom. "Make sure you don't call or speak to me for at least two weeks."

CHAPTER 22

Stacy had a meeting in her craft room. At the meeting were Crystal, Landon, Heather, (Briggs' mom) Briggs, Tracey, Carley, Sydney, and Cole.

"I'm reading what was in the newspaper this morning." Stacy read the two newspaper articles.

After reading the articles, she stated, "A lot of the dogs had rewards. The authorities divided it equally among the kids. She gave each child an envelope with a check enclosed. When they opened the envelopes and saw the checks, Sydney, Carley, and Cole squealed. Briggs and Landon asked, "How much?"

Carley excitedly yelled, "It's for $500."

"Wow," said Landon. "We're rich."

"We sure are," agreed Briggs.

This is what the newspaper articles stated:

DOG FIGHTING RING CLOSED

Five minor children exposed a dognapping and illegal dog fighting ring in Loranger. We are withholding the names of the perpetrators until we have all information. We will give only the first names of the dogs' rescuers, due to the fact that they are all minors.

They are: Cole, Sydney, Carley, Landon and Briggs. Without them, many more pets would have endured the agony and inhumane treatment of the dognappers. All

these minor children are heroes in the eyes of the owners
of pets that were stolen.

HARMONY ACRES CLOSED

Due to the illegal operation of the owners of Harmony
Acres, the business is now closed. It seemed as though
they lured the unsuspecting victims to the clinic under
the false pretense of being a retreat. It supposedly had
amenities, such as: relaxing atmosphere, spa, massage,
sauna, and more. The victims were charged a fee for this
fabulous service.

In fact, it was a place in which the victims were shot
up with sedatives and physically abused.

Once the victims were allowed to leave, they were too
fearful to say anything about their experiences.

The owners told the insurance companies that the
victims were patients. The owners collected insurance
payments until the insurance payments reached the
maximum amount of coverage. The owners of Harmony
Acres are facing multiple criminal charges.

CHAPTER 23

A COUPLE OF WEEKS LATER, Carley and Sydney were in the craft room decorating boxes. That was another thing they did for extra money.

Stacy came to the door and said, "Your cousin Evie is here."

Donna and Evie came to the door. Donna said, "Hey, girls. What you been up to?"

Sydney and Carley were always happy to see their Aunt Donna. Donna is the first cousin of Debbie (Carley's grandmother), Linda (Sydney's grandmother a/k/a Granny Nanny), and Crystal (Landon's grandmother).

Granny Nanny was in the kitchen drinking iced tea. Donna and Stacy went back into the kitchen.

Evie (nickname for Evangeline) stayed in the craft room and watched as Carley and Sydney were putting the finishing touches on the boxes.

When they were finished, Carley asked, "What would you like to do, Evie? Would you like to do some crafts? You want to decorate a box?"

Evie held her head down and didn't speak.

"What's wrong, Evie," asked Sydney.

Evie whispered, "I need help."

Carley and Sydney looked at each other.

Sydney put her head in her hand and thought, *Oh, no. Not again.*

CPSIA information can be obtained
at www.ICGtesting.com
Printed in the USA
LVHW011658181122
733278LV00019B/1133

9 781977 258571